My Dog

Written by
Judy Taylor

Illustrated by
Reg Cartwright

WALKER BOOKS
LONDON

My dog was given to me ...

and he was beautiful.

My dog slept in a basket...

until he ate it.

My dog chewed his bone…

and then buried it.

My dog made a friend...

and then chased her.

My dog played with his ball..

until he lost it.

My dog goes for walks…

and loves it.

My dog has a bath…

and hates it.

My dog goes to sleep…

and dreams.

MORE WALKER PAPERBACKS

THE PRE-SCHOOL YEARS

John Satchwell
& Katy Sleight
Monster Maths
ODD ONE OUT   BIG AND LITTLE
COUNTING   SHAPES

FOR THE VERY YOUNG

Byron Barton
TRAINS   TRUCKS   BOATS
AEROPLANES

PICTURE BOOKS
For All Ages

Colin West
"HELLO, GREAT BIG BULLFROG!"
"PARDON?" SAID THE GIRAFFE
"HAVE YOU SEEN THE CROCODILE?"
"NOT ME," SAID THE MONKEY

Bob Graham
THE RED WOOLLEN BLANKET

Russell Hoban
& Colin McNaughton
The Hungry Three
THEY CAME FROM AARGH!
THE GREAT FRUIT GUM ROBBERY

Jill Murphy
FIVE MINUTES' PEACE

Philippa Pearce
& John Lawrence
EMILY'S OWN ELEPHANT

David Lloyd
& Charlotte Voake
THE RIDICULOUS STORY OF
GAMMER GURTON'S NEEDLE

Nicola Bayley
Copycats
SPIDER CAT   PARROT CAT
POLAR BEAR CAT   ELEPHANT CAT
CRAB CAT

Michael Rosen
& Quentin Blake
Scrapbooks
SMELLY JELLY SMELLY JELLY
(THE SEASIDE BOOK)
HARD-BOILED LEGS
(THE BREAKFAST BOOK)
SPOLLYOLLYDIDDLYTIDDLYITIS
(THE DOCTOR BOOK)
UNDER THE BED
(THE BEDTIME BOOK)

Jan Ormerod
THE STORY OF CHICKEN LICKEN

Bamber Gascoigne
& Joseph Wright
BOOK OF AMAZING FACTS 1

Martin Handford
WHERE'S WALLY?